W9-AYD-801

excellent Emma

OTHER BOOKS ABOUT EMMA

x x x

Only Emma

Not-So-Weird Emma

Super Emma

Best Friend Emma

excellent Emma

saLLy WaRNeR

Illustrated by

jamie HaRpeR

Viking

Franklin Library
Summit Public Schools

Viking

Published by Penguin Group

Penguin Young Readers Group, 345 Hudson Street, New York, New York 10014, U.S.A.

Penguin Group (Canada), 90 Eglinton Avenue East, Suite 700, Toronto,

Ontario, Canada M4P 2Y3 (a division of Pearson Penguin Canada Inc.)

Penguin Books Ltd, 80 Strand, London WC2R 0RL, England

Penguin Ireland, 25 St Stephen's Green, Dublin 2, Ireland (a division of Penguin Books Ltd)

Penguin Group (Australia), 250 Camberwell Road, Camberwell, Victoria 3124, Australia

(a division of Pearson Australia Group Pty Ltd)

Penguin Books India Pvt Ltd, 11 Community Centre, Panchsheel Park,

New Delhi – 110 017, India

Penguin Group (NZ), 67 Apollo Drive, Rosedale, North Shore 0632,

New Zealand (a division of Pearson New Zealand Ltd)

Penguin Books (South Africa) (Pty) Ltd, 24 Sturdee Avenue, Rosebank,

Johannesburg 2196, South Africa

Penguin Books Ltd, Registered Offices: 80 Strand, London WC2R 0RL, England

First published in 2009 by Viking, a division of Penguin Young Readers Group

1 3 5 7 9 10 8 6 4 2

Text copyright © Sally Warner, 2009
Illustrations copyright © Jamie Harper, 2009
All rights reserved

LIBRARY OF CONGRESS CATALOGING-IN-PUBLICATION DATA IS AVAILABLE
ISBN: 978-0-670-06310-9

Manufactured in China

For the excellent Jane Willi—S.W.

x   x   x

For Ros—J.H.

Contents

excellent Emma

✕ 1 ✕
Ka-pow!

Ka-pow!

"Take that, Lettice Wallingford," I whisper under my breath—and the liquidambar pod bounces away toward Oak Glen Primary School, where I am in the third grade.

I aim the scuffed toe of my red sneaker at the small pod—which is also called a sweet-gum ball, even though that name is like cheating, because it makes the spiky pod sound like something good to eat—and I kick it again, as hard as I can.

Lettice. What a stupid name, I think, as I watch the pod roll to a stop in front of me on the sidewalk. "Hello, my name is Lettice," I say in a fakey-

English voice, trying it out. "And these are my best friends, Asparagus and Baked Potato."

Lettice Wallingford is eight years old, just like me. She is fancy Annabelle's favorite English niece. Annabelle is my dad's new English wife. Well, she's not so new anymore, I remind myself, taking aim at the pod again, because they've been married for two years, ever since I was six. They get to live in London, England, while I, Emma McGraw, am stuck here with my mom in boring old Oak Glen, California.

Lettice is "almost like a daughter" to Annabelle, my dad keeps telling me. And pretty soon, Lettice will probably start seeming like a daughter to *him*.

Ka-pow!

Lettice probably thinks she's so great, just because she's a champion horseback rider who won a silver cup last weekend. My dad told me all about it in his latest e-mail, like he thought I'd be interested.

Thanks, *Dad*. That was just what I needed to read on my computer screen on a rainy December night.

"I could win a silver cup if *I* had a beautiful horse," I say under my breath. "Anyone could, probably. That's not so wonderful."

But my dad—who I haven't even seen for eight months!—seems to think it is extremely wonderful, and that Lettice and I would really, really like each other.

"Right, like Lettice Wallingford is so amazing," I say sarcastically, kicking the poor innocent pod once more. "Just because she has a horse, and she is probably really cute, and she speaks with an English accent.

"I *hate* her," I whisper, and hot tears fill my eyes.

Well, maybe I can't really blame Lettice for her accent, I think, trying to be a little bit fair. After all, she lives in Engand. They probably don't even call it an English accent there. They just called it *talking*.

Ka-pow!

"I still hate her," I decide, and I wipe a tear away with the back of my hand. "Lettice is a champion now, and I'll bet she gets to see my dad all the time, because of stupid, fancy Annabelle. They probably have tea parties together, with chocolate cupcakes, my favorite. And now Daddy is going to start comparing me to Lettice," I tell myself. "And I'm not that good at *anything*. Anything that shows, anyway. How am I supposed to compete?"

Grown-ups don't hand out silver cups to a kid just because she wants to be a nature scientist when she grows up. Or because she's brave when her parents get divorced and her father moves to a whole different country.

Ka-pow!

"What are you doing?" a croaky voice asks, seeming to come out of nowhere. "Trying to kick the spiky ball all the way to school?"

It is EllRay Jakes, the smallest kid in my third-grade class. I am only second smallest, which is something to be grateful for, I guess. "Maybe I am," I tell him. "I wasn't really thinking about it. You can have it, if you want."

"But *we're* almost there," he says, pointing to the school's crowded front steps.

"So don't take it," I tell him, shrugging. "I don't care if you want it or not."

"I didn't say I didn't want it," EllRay tells me quickly, and he picks up the battered spiky ball and jams it into his backpack, which already looks full. "Thanks, Emma."

"Oh, leave me alone!" I say. All of a sudden, I am pretty sure I am about to start crying again, because EllRay's friendly, smiling face is only making things worse. And crying is something I could never live down at school.

It isn't even eight thirty in the morning yet! This is going to be a lo-o-o-ong day.

"Hey, what'd I do?" EllRay asks, confused. "You can have it back if you—"

"I said, leave me *alone*," I shout, and I start running as fast as I can toward the school's front steps.

And that's pretty fast!

typicaL Boy Behavior

"Why can't you come to my birthday party? I don't get it," Jared says to Corey on the playground that same afternoon. But he sounds mad, not sad. Sad is definitely the way a girl would sound in the same situation.

It is recess, but my best friend, Annie Pat Masterson, and I didn't feel like running around on the still wet playground or hanging on the cold, drippy chain-link fence like the other girls in my class, even though most of them are nice, especially Kry Rodriguez. Instead, we are practicing making faces at each other at the third-grade picnic table. But the boys are goofing around and talking under a nearby tree, so we have also been listening to what they're saying.

As future nature scientists, Annie Pat and I have noticed that a group of boys can easily ignore one or two girls, but three or more girls make them nervous. Then, they become as alert as a herd of zebras when a bunch of lionesses go strolling by.

It is windy and cool out today, the first Monday in December. I am wearing my new green sweater, and Annie Pat is wearing her very cute red hoodie, which matches her hair almost perfectly, but the boys are not noticing us at all. Eavesdropping conditions are ideal!

"Why won't you come to my birthday?" Jared asks again, scowling at Corey.

"I told you," Corey says, sounding nervous. "I have swim practice that afternoon. There's this big meet coming up in January. My mom says we're still gonna get you a present, though, so don't worry." He ruffles his hand through his white-blond hair.

"But you *always* have swim practice," Jared argues, ignoring the part about the birthday present.

"Yeah," Stanley chimes in, loyal as ever to Jared. "Why do you have to keep practicing and practicing? Don't you already know how to swim? My mom says I'm a real good swimmer, and I'm going."

Stanley might know how to swim, but it's different for Corey, I'm pretty sure. He is already a champion swimmer, and he's only going to get better as he grows up, our parents say. Although what you would do all day long as a grown-up swimming champion, I don't know.

"Hey, Stanley," EllRay Jakes says. "Can you stick your tongue out like this? Like a tube? Watch me!"

Boys like to try to do crazy things with their

bodies. Annie Pat and I look at each other and start to crack up—but *silently*. We don't want to waste this opportunity to study another species at close range.

"No, I can't," Stanley says, not even trying. "But I can wiggle my ears and bend the tops of my fingers funny."

"I can stick out *my* tongue like a tube," Corey tells them.

"Shut up," Jared says, still angry about the party. "You think you're better than us, just because you win prizes for swimming, and—"

"You shut up," EllRay interrupts, even though Jared wasn't talking to him, and even though EllRay is small and Jared is big. But EllRay and Corey are friends.

"My cousin broke two of his fingers playing basketball," Kevin reports. This news comes completely out of nowhere. "And now one of them is bent funny *forever*."

"You liar," Jared says. "You don't even *have* a cousin who plays basketball."

"Yeah, I do," Kevin tells him, almost apologetic. "He lives in Idaho, dude. His name's Bryan McKinley, and I can prove it. Ask my mom, if you don't believe me."

"Well, how come I never met him?" Jared asks, outraged.

"There's dinosaur tracks in Idaho," EllRay says,

excited. "Or somewhere like Idaho. I saw a picture once."

Now, this is typical boy behavior, to forget all about birthday parties and hurt feelings and broken fingers and being called a liar just because you happen to be reminded of some oddball fact— if EllRay's even telling the truth, which he might not be. Maybe he's just trying to change the subject to avoid a fight, which would actually be pretty smart.

"I don't know," Stanley says, sounding doubtful. "Bryan never said anything about there being any *dinosaurs* in Idaho. And I saw him on the fourth of July."

"They're not real dinosaurs, dummy," Corey says, laughing.

"You mean they're fake dinosaur tracks?" Stanley says. "What's so great about that?"

"Even I could make fake dinosaur tracks," Kevin says. And he's probably already planning how to do it—just to impress Jared.

"They're real tracks, but they're from a long time ago," EllRay says stubbornly. "I don't know what kind of dinosaur it was, though."

"Well, I know they're not pterodactyl tracks," Jared says in a loud voice, eager to be boss of the conversation once more. He is an expert on dinosaurs, to hear him tell it. "Because pterodactyls fly, so they never leave footprints on the ground. They probably don't even have feet." He says this as if the prehistoric creatures are still buzzing around, bumping into helicopters and stuff.

By now, Annie Pat and I can barely keep from giggling out loud.

"They had to land some-time," EllRay insists.

"Nuh-uh," Jared says.

"Then pterodactyls are like hummingbirds," Kevin says, suddenly pretending to be the expert. "*Big* hummingbirds.

Hummingbirds are the only birds that can fly backwards and upside down.

Because if a hummingbird stops flying, it dies."

Now, I happen to know that's not true, because I've seen hummingbirds sitting on flowers and telephone wires lots of times. Not for very long, true, but they were definitely alive while they were sitting there.

Kevin sounds pretty sure of himself, though, so no one argues with him. "Yeah," Jared finally says. "Pterodactyls are exactly like humming-birds."

I don't think even Kevin believes this one, but the boys' conversation seems to have run out of fuel. A few of them are finally eating their snacks and are too busy to talk.

"So what are you getting me for my birthday?" Jared asks Corey.

"Huh?"

"You said your mom was still gonna get me a present even though you can't come to my party," Jared reminds him.

"Oh, yeah," Corey says. "Well, I don't know yet. But it'll be something really good, so don't worry."

"I'm not worried," Jared tells him.

"Yeah," Kevin chimes in. "Like Jared's so *worried*."

"I don't get it, though," Jared says. "If you really wanted to come to my party you would. And it's gonna be great! So how come you won't be there?"

And—the boys are back where they started. Each boy said what he wanted to say, and nobody's crying or mad, and they're all still friends, pretty much.

That's actually a very good thing about boys.

It's the exact opposite with girls. I *guarantee* there was some girl-drama out on the playground or at the chain-link fence this recess, and both Annie Pat and I will hear about it within five minutes of sitting down in Ms. Sanchez's

class, even though we're all supposed to be perfectly quiet.

And that drama won't be over for at least a
week.

But the bell's about to ring.

Br–r–r–r–r–n–n–n–n–g!

x **3** x

Good at Something

"There will be a big announcement at the end of class," our teacher, Ms. Sanchez, tells us with a mysterious smile. "But for now, please hand out the rulers, Stanley. And Heather, kindly pass out the boxes of colored markers," she adds. A *this-is-going-to-be-fun!* look is on her face. "It's time for art."

Ms. Sanchez is the prettiest teacher at Oak Glen Primary School, which is only one reason we're lucky to have her. She pulls her shiny black hair back into a soft bun, and she wears really cute clothes. A second reason we're lucky to have her as our teacher is that she's nice, and a third reason is that she's engaged, which is fun for us to talk about when things get boring. Fun for the girls, anyway.

In fact, Ms. Sanchez is *so* engaged that her twinkly diamond ring nearly hypnotizes her, she looks at it so much! She also reads a lot of magazines about brides. The girls all want to get invited to her wedding, whenever it will be, but my mom says we shouldn't get our hopes up.

I am *always* getting my hopes up—about everything. Why not? It's free!

And it's fun.

Annie Pat has been a little more cautious recently about getting *her* hopes up about things, but I think that's probably because her mom just had a baby. Annie Pat is tired from all the crying at night, in my opinion.

The man Ms. Sanchez is going to marry is named Mr. Timberlake, but he's not the same Mr. Timberlake who's on MTV. *Her* Mr. Timberlake works in a sporting-goods store. Kevin says he and his dad bought a baseball bat from him once, but I think Kevin made that up.

Mr. Timberlake is as handsome as Ms. Sanchez is beautiful, thank goodness. They match.

The coolest thing so far about Ms. Sanchez and Mr. Timberlake is that one time they went skydiving together. Nobody in class actually saw them do it, but it's true, because she told us. In fact, the boys in our class are hoping that Ms. Sanchez marries Mr. Timberlake up in the air, halfway between the airplane and the ground!

I think that would be a dumb thing to do, and also very dangerous. There would have to be a minister jumping out of the plane, too, to marry them, and a fourth person to take pictures.

And Ms. Sanchez's beautiful lacy veil might get tangled up in all those parachute strings. The whole wedding could easily be a *disaster*, and that is no way to start being married! Being married seems to be hard enough when you start out the normal way—judging from my own mom and dad, who got divorced when I was two.

I hate divorce, which is why I'm never getting married.

Annie Pat's parents seem happy, though. So far, so good, anyway.

Since it's Friday today, Ms. Sanchez has obviously decided to squeeze in an art lesson instead of trying to teach us Spanish, which is what she usually does on Friday afternoons. At this school, it's music and art on Fridays—but only when there's nothing better to do. That's the way they look at things here in Oak Glen, I guess.

My old school was Magdalena, which was girls only. Magdalena is twenty miles away from Oak Glen Primary School, but it might as well be a million miles away, and not just in distance. At Magdalena, we got to have music and art every single week. Orchestra *and* chorus! Painting *and* drawing *and* collage *and* ceramics!

But then my mom lost her job as librarian for a big company two years ago, right about the time Dad got remarried, and Mom and I had to sell our house and move to a condo in Oak Glen to save money. Now Mom works at home correcting things other people write. She says she likes it okay, though.

Ms. Sanchez probably feels guilty because our class hasn't done any art at all since Thanksgiving, when we each used a pattern to cut out an autumn leaf for a fluttery Open House tree—which, I heard from a fourth-grader, is something that Ms. Sanchez's class does every year. And then we wrote our names on the leaves in our most perfect cursive, and we got to use glitter paint, even though you can tell Ms. Sanchez hates glitter, because it gets all over the place. And she also hates glue bottles, because they're always stopped up.

I don't exactly call construction-paper leaves *art*, however. It is just cutting on the line, really—which most kids learn to do pretty well when they're four or five.

Ms. Sanchez isn't that great at art, to tell the truth. It's one of her few faults. She either has us do an easy holiday craft project, the kind you see in magazines—only our projects never come out looking right—or she teaches us the color wheel.

Over and over again.

"Now, use your rulers to draw a big triangle," she calls out.

The color wheel. I could do this in my sleep!

"Excuse me, excuse me," Heather says, waving her hand in the air so much that her ponytail bounces. Heather usually also has one long skinny braid hanging down over her face for decoration, and it is swinging today like a skinny little vine in the Amazon jungle, which is a place I want to go to study nature someday. I love the Amazon! Except for giant snakes like the anaconda, but I am trying—not very hard, I admit—to get over that. "What color do you want the triangle to be this time?" Heather asks.

Some anacondas are so big they can eat small alligators.

Heather likes to get things exactly right, and she's not the only one. Cynthia Harbison is even worse, and so are the two girls who are best friends from church. I'm not that "persnickety," to use one of my mom's favorite words, unless it's about something important,

like nature. Or dinner. I can be *wa–a–a–y* persnickety then.

Don't try to sneak any lima beans past me,
that's all I'm saying.

Or brussels sprouts.

"The triangle can be any color at all, Heather,"
Ms. Sanchez says, but her face pinches up a little
at the words *this time.*

I don't mind repeating boring assignments,
though, even when they're in a subject that's
supposed to be fun, like art. That's because boring assignments give me a chance to think,
which is something you almost never get to do
in school. And what I am thinking about right
now is Corey Robinson, and how he's so good at
swimming.

I wish *I* was good at something. I mean, really
good at something people could actually see. Not
just knowing stuff about nature, because like I
said before, that's invisible.

I want to be good at something that will impress my dad.

In fact, I want to be *excellent*.

"Emma?" Ms. Sanchez is saying.

"Yes!" I shout, jumping in my seat at the sound of her voice, which makes Cynthia snicker loud enough for a few kids to hear.

"I was asking you what the complementary color of blue is," Ms. Sanchez says, sounding a little fakey-patient, to tell the truth.

Complementary means *opposite*, on the color wheel. I don't know why.

"Orange," I say automatically.

"That's correct," she says, smiling and surprised. "And I thought you weren't paying attention."

So I sit up straighter in my chair and try to look as though I *am* paying attention—because I like Ms. Sanchez that much.

Also, I want her to finish this lesson so we can hear the mysterious big announcement.

x 4 x

is that a threat or a promise?

"And now, boys and girls," Ms. Sanchez says after the last ruler and marker have been put away, "we have a special visitor who has something really fun to share with us." I sneak a look at the wall clock and see that there are only twenty minutes left in the school day.

The classroom door opens a little. "Please welcome our wonderful room mother, EllRay's mom, Mrs. Jakes," Ms. Sanchez says, and Mrs. Jakes walks into the our room. She is medium-brown like EllRay, and she has sparkling eyes, and short hair with lots of pretty curls in it, but she looks nervous.

And we're just a bunch of third-graders!

EllRay looks surprised, proud, and embarrassed—all at the same time—the way any kid would if their mom or dad came to class.

"Hello, boys and girls," Mrs. Jakes says, standing next to Ms. Sanchez at the front of the class.

"Hello," our combined raggedy voices mumble back at her.

EllRay's mom clears her throat. "The PTA has decided that we should all be doing more to encourage active lifestyles among the kids at Oak Glen," she announces, and she gives us a great big encouraging smile.

Active lifestyles. Oh, I think suddenly—this idea probably came from one of those *kids-are-too-fat-and-lazy-today!* reports they keep showing on TV. I can just picture all the grown-ups in the PTA—the Parent Teacher Association—sitting around eating squares of sheet cake while they talk about it.

People like to be experts about everybody else, that's what I think.

"A week from this Friday," Ms. Jakes says, "Oak Glen Primary School will be starting a new tradition. We will have our First Annual Winter Games Day. All the parents and grandparents will be invited, and it promises to be a lot of fun."

A puzzled silence fills the room, and EllRay sinks lower in his chair. "Winter Games Day?" Fiona asks. You mean like— like skiing? Because I have really, really weak ankles, and—"

"And it never snows in Oak Glen," Heather says, as if she is finishing Fiona's sentence. "This is Southern California. With palm trees," she reminds everyone. Heather is the queen of saying the most obvious thing in the world.

"But we still have winter, don't forget," Kry Rodriguez points out. Kry is really pretty, and her long straight bangs fall past her eyebrows and almost hide her eyes. Her parents are divorced, too, but that's not the only reason we're friends.

"One at a time, please," Ms. Sanchez reminds us. "And raise your hand if you have something to contribute."

Heather Patton raises her hand, and Ms. Sanchez tries to hide her sigh. "Yes, Heather?" she says, sounding patient.

Heather stands up as if she is about to pledge her allegiance. "I want to contribute a question," she says, "which is, what kind of stuff are they going to make us do on games day?"

"Good question, Heather," Ms. Sanchez says with fake enthusiasm, probably trying to make up for her sigh.

"It's not all firmed up yet," Mrs. Jakes says, "but of course there will be the usual foot races, and distance jumping, and so on. And some special competitions we're thinking of just for that one afternoon."

Cynthia Harbison frowns. "But we're all gonna win a prize, right?" she ask. "That's my contribution," she adds hastily, seeing Ms. Sanchez's expression.

"Well, yes," EllRay's mom says, sounding a little uncertain. "You'll win a prize if you win one of the contests. I'm afraid the PTA can't afford prizes for *everyone*."

"We should win something

just for trying," Stanley Washington says, keeping his voice low.

"Yeah," Heather chimes in.

"Hands in the air if you have a *contribution*," Ms. Sanchez reminds us icily. But no more hands go up. "Was there anything else, Mrs. Jakes?" Ms. Sanchez asks, smiling her encouragement.

"I think that's pretty much it," EllRay's mom says, looking a little flustered. "I mean, as Krysten said, we do have winter here in Oak Glen, even if it doesn't snow. And the school board decided that Winter Games Day would be a fun way for all the children in our school to enjoy some much-needed exercise."

"They think we're too fat," Stanley announces gloomily. "That's why they're punishing us." Stanley is a little pudgy around the middle, I guess, but I would never call him fat. Not out loud. And anyway, a bunch of the kids in our class are skinny, so it kind of evens out.

"They can't make us do stuff we don't want to do," Cynthia announces, raising her hand mid-sentence. She folds her arms across her chest. *"I'm not too fat."*

"Don't be silly," Ms. Sanchez says to everyone, scowling. She is obviously not at all happy that Mrs. Jakes's so-called exciting announcement has been met with such suspicion.

Mrs. Jakes looks as if she wishes she could turn back time and say things in a different way, but she doesn't know how.

Well, turning back time is impossible, for one thing.

"For heaven's sake, boys and girls!" Ms. Sanchez exclaims. "The parents are going to a great deal of trouble to make this new event a success, and it'll be fun for you. Just because it will actually involve *moving around*, weak ankles or not, instead of eating fast food or playing video games, that's no reason for you to give Mrs. Jakes and me all this attitude.

You kids are going to participate in Oak Glen's First Annual Winter Games Day, and you will like it!"

Annie Pat and I exchange looks. *Wow,* we are saying silently to each other. *Is that a threat or a promise?*

Naturally, we don't ask this question out loud, however, because Ms. Sanchez—who hardly ever gets mad—is *angry.* Her cheeks are pink, and her brown eyes flash, and one foot—wearing a pointy brown shoe with a cute leather bow on it—is tapping pretty hard.

No one else is reckless enough to say anything, either.

Except for Fiona. "I really do have weak ankles," she objects. She holds one leg up as a visual aid, and we all stare.

Her ankle does look kind of flimsy, now that

she mentions it—like a pink pipe cleaner with a lime-green sneaker stuck on the end of it.

"Well, Miss McNulty," Ms. Sanchez tells her, "you'd better get those ankles pumped up, and pumped up fast—because Winter Games Day is going to come rolling around next week whether you children want it to or not."

A couple of kids wriggle in their seats, but that's as far as they dare to go with their objections. The rest of us just stare at our shoes.

"Now, I want you to give a big Oak Glen thank-you to Mrs. Jakes for taking time out of her busy day to bring us this good news," Ms. Sanchez says in her best *I'm warning you!* voice.

"Thank you, Mrs. Jakes," a few of us manage to chant.

"You're welcome, everyone," EllRay's mom

says, and she leaves the classroom as quickly as she can while still being polite.

Then the bell rings, and we all slink out of the room.

And EllRay is the slinkiest of us all, because it was *his mom*.

𝒳 5 𝒳

iN trAiNiNG

"You're up early for a Saturday morning, Emma," Mom says a few days later, pouring herself some coffee. Coffee always looks so good, all steamy in the morning sunlight, but it tastes awful, which I know because I tried it once. "And you're already dressed, surprise surprise," she adds. "What would you like for breakfast?"

My mom is really nice, and she's pretty, too, even though she's almost thirty-five years old. She has short hair that waves up like the back end of a curly-tailed mallard duck, and

Ducks can sleep standing on one foot and with one eye open.

she likes to wear necklaces. When I was little, I made her a dyed macaroni necklace once, orange and blue and lumpy—even *I* thought it looked kind of weird—and she wore it to work! Of course she worked in a business library then, so not too many people saw her.

Still.

"I'd like pancakes and oatmeal, please," I say, doing some stretches before sitting down at the kitchen table. I tuck my napkin into my jeans so I won't have to scramble around on the floor looking for it in a minute or two. Somebody should invent magnetic napkins, that's what I think.

"Pancakes *and* oatmeal?" my mom asks, raising an eyebrow. "Good heavens, Emma. Are you about to go into hibernation?"

"Nope," I tell her. "I'm about to go into

training—with Annie Pat, only she doesn't know it yet. There's going to be a games day at school next Friday, see, and Annie Pat and I are going to *rule*. We have a head start, because we're already skinny. I'm going over to her house right after I finish my chores, if that's okay, and we'll go to the park so we can practice."

The pancake mix is already halfway out of the cupboard, but Mom stops and frowns. "Back up a second," she says. "Skinny? I got the e-mail memo about Winter Games Day yesterday, Emma, and it didn't say anything about kids having to be skinny. In fact, that's not the idea at all."

"Huh," I say politely. Because that's the kind of thing grown-ups tell you even when the opposite is true.

I know that Annie Pat must be as excited about games

day as I am, because she loves prizes and awards of any kind. In fact, one whole corner of her bedroom is full of the things she's won: a little "Congratulations!" trophy from when she graduated from preschool, her "Sweetest Smile" certificate from kindergarten, her "Perfect Penmanship" award from first grade, and the "Most Improved Spelling" award from second grade.

And that's not even counting her prizes and ribbons and plaques from pre-ballet, gymnastics, soccer, and summer camp, where she got an award with glitter on it for "Best Dog Paddle."

Annie Pat has led a very accomplished life so far.

Not me. I just have one second-place ribbon from the second-grade spelling bee at Magdalena, and one certificate from Parks and Recreation—near my old house—for being able to tread water for two minutes without drowning. But they spelled my last name wrong: Macgraw, not McGraw.

It was still me gasping and splashing in that swimming pool, though.

"Well, of course, there will be prizes—for the winners," Mom says, flopping some pancake mix into a bowl. "But really, Emma," she continues, temporarily stalled in her pancake-making project, "at the end of Winter Games Day, everyone is supposed to end up feeling more positive about exercise, and realize how good it makes their bodies feel. Whatever size they are," my mom adds, frowning a little.

"I guess you're right," I say, as if she has just totally convinced me that fat or skinny, fast or slow, winner or loser, prize or no prize, everybody at Oak Glen Primary School is going to be perfectly happy at the end of its First Annual Winter Games Day.

Hah.

⅗ ⅗ ⅗

Two hours later, my mom and I have finished our Saturday chores. We changed the sheets and towels, did a few loads of laundry in our horrible condo laundry room that smells like a combination of bleach, yucky-sweet fabric softener, and cat pee—even though no one is allowed to have pets, so that smell is a mystery. We also watered all the house plants and cleaned out the refrigerator, even the vegetable drawer, which sometimes has scary-looking bags of green goo hiding in the bottom.

Cucumbers, probably. We always forget to eat them, and that is their revenge.

The six blocks from Candelaria Road, where our condo is, to Annie Pat Masterson's house at 315 Sycamore Lane is usually a fun and easy walk. Today, though, thanks to the PTA, I am thinking about this walk as *exercise*, which makes it seem like I'm doing another chore. I even ask my mom to drive me, since I don't want to start my official training until Annie Pat and I get to the park, but Mom says no.

"Okay, okay," I tell her, sounding grouchy. "I'll *walk*. Even though I won't get a prize."

"You bet your buttons you'll walk," Mom says, laughing. "It's a beautiful sunny day, Emma. And the fresh air and exercise will do you good." Grown-ups always say stuff like that. Usually while they're sitting inside, by the way.

"It's windy out," I complain, not wanting to give in so easily. "My hair will get all tangled up."

This is not a very good argument, because my hair is *already* tangled up. It always is. Annie Pat and Kry say my hair is pretty, but it is so curly and long that it hurts—or *something* hurts, maybe it's my brain—whenever my mom tries to comb it after a shampoo. And the wind will only make my hair situation worse.

But the wind makes no difference to animals. They always look perfect! This is just one more example of how great animals are. If people had fur instead of hair, we'd be a lot better off.

"Don't worry," Mom tells me. "I'll brush your hair smooth when you get home. Maybe we'll even go out for a pizza tonight! Let's live it up for once."

"Oka-a-ay, but don't forget that I'm in training," I say slowly, not wanting her to think she can win me over with mere pizza.

Although, of course, she can.

✕ 6 ✕

Best Friends

Eucalyptus leaves rustle above me as I walk down Candelaria Road. They release a strong cough–drop smell that makes me want to sneeze.

I like sneezing. It's fun, if you have a tissue handy.

A few dried leaves tumble past my feet as I hurry down the sidewalk. Sometimes, when the wind blows like this, I feel like I am flying instead of walking. With each step I take, I bounce a little higher.

It would be so wonderful to be a kangaroo on a day like today! That's the kind of mom I'd like to be someday, too, because kangaroos are mar-

A kangaroo can't walk without using its tail for balance.

supials, and a marsupial's baby grows inside her pouch instead of in her belly.

It's a much better system than the human method, in my opinion.

I like going over to Annie Pat's for many reasons. For one thing, it's a house, like Mom and I used to have, not a condo like we live in now. Sometimes I even pretend Annie Pat's house *is* my house, and I have a mom and dad who live together in it. Undivorced.

But I don't tell Annie Pat that. Even best friends keep some things private.

Another reason I like going over to Annie Pat's is because the Mastersons have a baby named Murphy, and he has red hair just like Annie Pat. Murphy is fun to watch, and he's so new that he doesn't bother us yet.

Another good thing about Annie Pat's house is that her mom has to take care of Murphy all the time, so she leaves Annie Pat and me alone pretty much. And she buys really yummy snacks for us to eat, stuff I would never get at home. I think this is because she feels bad about ignoring Annie Pat ever since the baby showed up.

But I don't think Annie Pat minds a bit.

In my opinion, Murphy is all plusses and no minuses for Annie Pat and me.

But the main reason I like going to Annie Pat's house is because of Annie Pat herself. Like I said before, she is my best friend at Oak Glen, and Kry Rodriguez is my second-best friend, even though I would never say that out loud. I am not a feelings-hurter, unlike some people I could mention.

Cynthia Harbison and Jared Matthews.

Annie Pat Masterson is the second-smallest girl in the third grade, after me, and she is very bouncy, and she blushes a lot. Her hair is red, like

I said before, and she wears it parted down the middle and pulled to each side in pigtails. She has navy blue eyes.

The best thing about Annie Pat, though, is that she loves nature, just like I do. In fact, she wants to be a marine biologist when she grows up. Well, she'd really like to be one *now*, only grown-ups don't let kids do cool stuff like that. They keep those jobs for themselves.

I want to be a nature scientist, as I mentioned before. I don't know yet what my specialty will be, but I've definitely eliminated reptiles, especially snakes and skinks. Also amphibians, even though it is extremely cool that they can breathe both underwater *and* on land. I wish I could do that!

I knock three times on the Mastersons' red front door.

Mrs. Masterson swings open the door and holds it with her hip. She has baby Murphy cradled against her stomach. There is a snail-trail of white goo decorating her saggy green turtleneck shirt.

No offense or any-
thing, but *eww*.

"Emma! Welcome,"
Mrs. Masterson says,
giving me a big old
smile—probably because
since *I'm* here, she's glad
she doesn't have to feel
bad anymore about
playing with Murphy
all day, and not Annie Pat.

"Hi," I reply, feeling shy as I try
to think of something polite to say.
"Murphy looks even bigger than the last
time I saw him."

"Oh," she says, and she turns Murphy around
to face me. "Well, he probably is. Say hello to
Emma, Murphy," she tells him. "*Hewwo*," she
says, pretending to be Murphy.

This is very embarrassing!

"Annie Pat's in her room," Mrs. Masterson

says. "She's still pretty pooped from last night, because this little fella kept us awake with his crying just about all night long. He's teething," she adds proudly, nuzzling his neck.

"Oh," I say. "That's good. That he's getting teeth, I mean, because he couldn't eat corn on the cob next summer if he didn't. Or even *off* the cob. Well, I'd better be going," I say, edging toward the hall. I am trying to escape to Annie Pat's room before Mrs. Masterson actually shows Murphy's new teeth to me.

I'm interested in them, but not *that* interested.

X X X

Annie Pat is so tired that even her hair is drooping. A shriveled-up cornflake is stuck to her pajama top. "Whoa," I say. "I guess your mom was telling the truth about last night."

"Course she was," Annie Pat says. "Whenever I

started to fall asleep, I would dream there were these cats outside, fighting. But it was always Murphy. He makes a lot of noise for such a little baby."

"But he's not crying now," I point out. "Why can't he cry during the day, when everyone's awake?"

"I don't know. Why don't you go ask him?" Annie Pat says, sounding a little sarcastic, in my opinion.

"Never mind," I say quickly. "The important thing is that we get started on our training. You know," I add, seeing the confused expression on Annie Pat's face, "for Winter Games Day. Let's go to the park and practice running or something."

"If I tried to run now, I'd just fall over and start snoring," Annie Pat informs me.

But she flicks a glance toward her awards corner, as if looking for empty spots.

"You'll wake up," I assure her. "Think of the prizes they'll be handing out next week!"

"Yeah, if you *win*," Annie Pat says. "You're better than I am at that kind of stuff, Emma. Admit it."

"No, I'm not," I tell her. "Well, maybe I'm a little better. But I could help you train."

"I wanted us to do something *fun* today," Annie Pat grumbles. "Like, we could look at the comic books my dad bought me. Or we could draw pictures, or play a board game. Or maybe watch a video."

"Watching a video isn't going to make us any stronger," I point out, also sounding grouchy— because Annie Pat talking about her father has made me remember *my* dad watching Lettice win her silver cup in London, England, last weekend.

And so I tell Annie Pat all about Lettice and my dad, because we're best friends.

Annie Pat is quiet for a couple of minutes. "I think maybe your dad was just trying to think of something to write in his e-mail," she finally tells me. "Or he wanted you to know how much he missed you. Or maybe that English girl is the only other kid he knows," she continues, "and he thought you'd want to hear about her, for some crazy reason. It's like when we go visit my aunt in Bakersfield, and she thinks I'm gonna love playing with her horrible next-door neighbor who stomps on snails—just because we're both eight years old. Yeah, right!"

"Maybe," I say slowly, thinking it over. "I don't know. My dad does keep saying he wants me to come visit him in England someday."

"There you go," Annie Pat says cheerily, pulling on her jeans. "He probably pictures you and Lettice going horseback riding together."

"Well, he can think again," I say, scowling. "I'm not going horseback riding with some—some *champion*, when I've only been on a horse once in my entire life, and that was a disaster, because my legs were so sore the whole next day that I walked like Frankenstein's monster. Do I want to look bad in front of my very own father?"

"I didn't think of that," Annie Pat says, her navy blue eyes wide.

"And I'm not gonna trot around after Lettice holding her stupid silver cup, either," I inform Annie Pat. "If *that's* what my dad has planned."

Mrs. Masterson pokes her head into Annie Pat's room. "Are you girls hungry for a snack?" she asks. "Because I have chocolate chip cookies in the kitchen, if anyone's interested."

Chocolate chip cookies! And it's only ten thirty in the morning! See what I mean?

"Want a cookie, Emma?" Annie Pat asks, tugging a sweatshirt over her head.

"No, thanks," I say reluctantly. "Because I'm in training."

I skip the part about going out for pizza with my mom tonight.

Mrs. Masterson looks surprised, probably because I have never before turned down a cookie, which is one of my favorite food groups.

"Well, *I* want a cookie," Annie Pat says, sounding

stubborn. "I'm not going to win any prizes next week anyway, so I have nothing to lose."

"Good! I'll pour you girls some orange juice, while I'm at it," her mom tells us. "And then I'm going to nap while the napping is good."

This must mean that Murphy is already asleep.

"Can Annie Pat and I go to the park this morning?" I ask quickly, before Mrs. Masterson disappears from Annie Pat's room.

"Hmmph," Annie Pat mumbles, irked that I have basically jumped a piece—like when you play checkers—and asked her mom this question when she, Annie Pat, should have been the one to do it—if she even wanted to go to the park, which she does not.

"I suppose so," Mrs. Masterson says, pausing in the doorway. "If you stick together. But be home in time for lunch, okay, sweetie?" she tells Annie Pat.

"Okay," Annie Pat says, sighing.

"I'll put your snack on the kitchen counter," Mrs. Masterson tells her. "And your nice healthy juice, Emma," she adds, turning to me.

I am already feeling sad about that lost cookie.

But I can't tell Annie Pat and her mom that I've changed my mind, can I?

There is such a thing as pride.

χ 7 χ

So Harsh

"Want to practice?" Kry Rodriguez asks a bunch of us on Tuesday, during afternoon recess. "If you jump downhill, you go farther," she confides, having just discovered this by making a spectacular leap that somehow ended in a graceful somersault.

But then, Kry is good—without even trying—at everything kids do outdoors, whether it's sports or playing, so it's not as if she needs those extra inches when she jumps downhill. Strange as it seems, I think she's actually trying to help the rest of us.

It is perfect outside today, cool and warm at the same time, and the wind is blowing the tree branches back and forth, and a few puffy white clouds are floating around in the sky. You would think it was an ideal day to jump and run, but *no-o-o-o*. That's not the way *some* kids see it. They are in a really terrible mood, and it's all because of Winter Games Day, which is on Friday afternoon.

Each of these gloomy kids sees this event as a bad thing, but for different reasons. Take Cynthia, for example. "No, I *don't* want to practice," she says, even though she usually kisses up to Kry a little. "If the PTA is too cheap to buy everyone prizes, why should we even bother?"

"Yeah," loyal Heather chimes in, because she usually kisses up to *Cynthia*. "They're just trying to make us feel bad about ourselves, that's what I think. And that's not very nice. I think maybe it's illegal, even."

"It's not the PTA's fault," EllRay mumbles, still sensitive about his mom being the one who made the announcement. "They can't help it if they're poor."

"It is so their fault," Stanley says. "They want us to make fools of ourselves in public—for nothing!"

"I wouldn't make a fool of myself even for *something*," Fiona McNulty says, shuddering. "But luckily I have an excuse for not trying. My ankles," she adds, reminding everyone. She waggles her feet as a visual aid. "But I think I should get a prize anyway, just for showing up," she says, trying out this idea on us.

"Good luck with that," Cynthia tells her, obviously not meaning it.

Other kids in my class—like me, and Annie Pat, too, I think, deep down inside—are looking forward to Winter Games Day, and it's for one reason: we think we're going to win something. Take Jared, for instance. "I'm not going to make a fool of *my*self," he announces proudly. "I'm going to run faster and jump farther than anyone, and I'll leave you guys in the dust. You're gonna be *amazed*."

"So why aren't you practicing, if you're such a champion?" Kry challenges him. Kry is the rare type of person who can say challenging stuff like that in a not-mean way. I don't know how she does it.

Jared blushes a little. "I want it to be a surprise, how good I am," he says.

"Yeah," Kevin McKinley says eagerly, pushing his glasses up. "Jared is going to be awesome, and he'll win every single prize."

"Even the *girl* prizes?" Cynthia teases, pretend-hiding her smile.

"Don't get your hopes up about that," EllRay

says. "Because I don't think there will be separate boy prizes and girl prizes. But if there are," he adds, sounding hopeful, "there should be tall prizes and short prizes, too, shouldn't there?"

"No one's as short as you, *EllRay*," Jared says. sounding bored and mean at the same time. "But don't worry," he adds. "Maybe they'll put you in with the first-graders, and then you'll stand a chance."

"Shut up," EllRay mumbles.

I feel bad for him, but I have learned not to try to defend boys. It only makes them mad.

"I think you're gonna do great," Corey tells Ell-Ray. "It'll be fun!"

"I don't care *what* the PTA says," Cynthia tells us, as if all the parents and teachers combined are standing right in front of her. "My mom says I'm a winner, and she and my dad are the only ones who get to vote."

"You *are* a winner," Heather agrees solemnly.

Next to me, my friend Annie Pat frowns. "Well, my mom says I'm a winner, too," she says, looking a little scared—as if Cynthia might be about to argue with her, or even challenge her to a duel to see who's *really* the winner. That would be a sight to see.

"Same here," Stanley says gloomily. "My mom and dad keep saying how good I am at everything, like that's gonna make it come true, and I'm just *not*. I mean, I'm good at some stuff, but not everything. Wait till they find out the truth about me—that I'm a loser, not a winner."

"Yeah, because parents will bring video cameras and everything," EllRay says. "They'll have proof of how bad you are, and that proof will last forever. It might even go on the Internet," he adds.

"You're good at eating, *Stanley*," Kevin points out, not in a nice way.

"Shut up."

"But everyone can't win," I say, trying to think

it through as I speak. "Not in an official, silver cup way, at least—or else winning wouldn't mean anything."

"You got that right, Emma," Heather says, flipping her little decoration braid back over her shoulder. "Someone's gotta be bad at stuff, and maybe it's you. And Annie Pat," she adds.

"Leave me out of this," Annie Pat mumbles.

"Corey is a winner," Kry says, after shooting Heather a warning look. "He's probably the only one here who's actually won *anything*. Anything real, anyway, from total strangers. And that's what counts."

We all turn to look at swimming champion Corey Robinson, who will probably be in the Olympics someday, a lot of people say. Corey blushes under his freckles and looks like he wishes he could disappear. "But it's different with swimming," he says, almost croaking out the words. "With swimming, you either come in first or you don't."

"That is so harsh," Heather says, her voice soft with sympathy.

"'*So harsh!*' Oh, I'm gonna hurl," Jared says, giving Corey—who is now even more embarrassed—a shove.

"Me, too," Kevin says. "Poor widdle Corey."

"Quit it," Corey says, trying to smile as he regains his balance. "*I* never said it was harsh."

"Let's run," Kry urges us again. "Let's do *something*, anyway."

"You have ants in your pants," Heather informs her. She is probably quoting her mom, who acts like this big expert on other people's kids. For example, there was the time during our school's open house that she told Mrs. Jakes in front of a bunch of other moms—and even some kids, including me—that she thought EllRay had ADD, and that's none of her business, if it's even true. "And it's cheating if you practice," Heather adds, making up this rule on the spot.

"*What?*" Kry says, as if she is about to start laughing.

"It is," Cynthia says, sounding sorry to have to break the news. "It's like trying too hard, Kry, and that's just lame. But that's okay. You're still kinda new. You didn't know."

Krysten frowns. "I don't think practicing is—"

"The bell's about to ring," Annie Pat interrupts, peering at her watch.

"Think fast," Jared says all of a sudden, bouncing a red kickball—which is supposed to be kept on the playground—off Fiona's head. He cackles out a laugh, and Stanley, Kevin, and Ell-Ray laugh, too.

"Ow-w-w-w," Fiona cries, clutching at her head. "Did it leave a mark?" she asks Heather, and Heather examines Fiona's head as if she's gathering evidence for a future lawsuit. The rest of us girls cluck our sympathy.

All but Kry Rodriguez, who has a better idea. She jumps to her feet and grabs the kickball. *"Think fast,"* she repeats to Jared, and she tosses the ball in the air—and then spikes it down harder than the best beach volleyball player you ever saw.

Wow!

The ball bounces off Jared's rear end with a hollow-sounding *thonk*, and EllRay has to scramble to recover it, Kry hit the ball so hard. "Hey," Jared yells, furious. He clutches at his rear like a cartoon guy who has just been stung by a wasp.

"Did you *see* that?" Stanley is whispering to Kevin. "That was awesome!"

"Sorry, Jared," Kry sings out, all innocent and everything. "My mistake. I thought you were ready for it!"

And Jared doesn't say a *word*.

8

tHiNK SLow

"Why so blue, sweetie?" Mom asks on Thursday night. "The weather forecast said the rain will stop by tomorrow, so Winter Games Day will go off without a hitch." I am curled up on our saggy green sofa with my head on a flowery pillow on Mom's lap, and we have both been reading library books. I'm collecting Required Reading Points, because I have to have at least forty by the end of January, but my mom gets to read just for fun.

Well, reading my book is fun, too. But when the grown-ups at Oak Glen turned reading—one of my favorite things—into points-gathering, they ruined it, in my opinion. That's probably the way Stanley felt when they turned exercise into "a punishment," as he put it.

Next thing you know, they'll tell us kids that our assignment is to *breathe*—and then we'll all want to hold our breath until we turn blue.

I tug the soft yellow blanket up to my chin and listen to the *tick-tick* of the rain outside and the *tick-tock* of the old clock on a nearby table. Every so often the wind swirls by, and the eucalyptus

trees creak and groan as if they are complaining about having to stay outside on such a miserable night.

Our house smells good, like the chicken tacos we had for dinner.

"Emma?" Mom asks softly, stroking my hair. "Are you asleep, honey?"

"Nuh-uh," I say, shaking my head a little. "I was just thinking about tomorrow."

"You must be feeling pretty good about things," Mom tells me. "What with all the preparation you've done."

Running and jumping are what Annie Pat and I have been practicing the most, in secret, because those are the two competitions Mrs. Jakes mentioned first.

"I think I'm better than I was a few days ago, anyway," I say. "And Annie Pat is running faster than she ever did before."

I am smiling under the blanket fringe, because I can't help but feel happy about how excellent we are going to be. *I hope*. I have a lot to prove to my dad, and Annie Pat would definitely like to add another prize to her collection.

She doesn't say so, but I know it's true.

"Your mind is racing, isn't it?" my mom says, shifting her legs a little and putting down her book.

"Yeah," I admit. "The boys in my class always say, *'Think fast!'* And I guess that's what I'm doing. Thinking fast."

Mom sighs. "I wish you could cool things down a little, Emma. I think you kids should tell each other to *think slow*. And in my humble opinion, you've got the whole spirit of Winter Games Day wrong. You're putting entirely too much emphasis on winning—or on other kids losing."

"But there are going to be prizes," I point out, feeling only a little bit sorry in advance for whoever-it-is who loses. "Someone has to come in last. And anyway, what's wrong with winning? You're always saying how special I am, Mom. Don't you want *proof*?"

"I certainly don't need proof that you're special, honey," my mom says, laughing. "But do you know who you remind me of?" she asks, stroking my tangled-up hair again.

"Who?"

"Me. When I was a little girl," Mom says, and I snuggle in for one of my favorite things in the world, a story about when she was a kid. Listening to her stories is like finding the lost pieces of a great big jigsaw puzzle. And when I finish the puzzle, I'll know exactly the kind of kid my mom used to be.

Will I ever finish that invisible puzzle?

I think she and I would have been friends, if I had been on the earth way back then. Maybe not *best* friends, because she is a lot neater than I am, but still.

"Tell," I say, shutting my eyes.

"Well," Mom says, thinking back, "when I was about nine, your grandmama was organizing a fashion show to raise money for some charity she was involved in. And she needed a few children to be models, so of course she signed me up."

"You were a *supermodel*?" I ask, impressed. "Wow! But I thought you told me once that you were a tomboy."

That's the weird-but-fun thing about my invisible mom-puzzle. Sometimes the pieces don't fit.

"They didn't have many supermodels back in those days," Mom tells me, laughing. "But in any case, I think you could have called me a not-so-super model that terrible afternoon. Because even though I wanted to make my mama proud, I experienced some—uh—technical difficulties."

"You did?"

Mom nods, solemn. "It all started with the outfit I was supposed to wear. You know how much your grandmama loves clothes, Emma."

It's true. Grandmama is a very dressed-up, old-fashioned lady. She lives far away in Michigan, and she sends me these weird outfits that no kid in California would ever wear.

Except I have to, when she comes to visit. It is always very embarrassing.

This is another good example of how fast my feelings sometimes change—from happiness that my grandmama is visiting, to horror that I have to go out in public wearing the clothes she's given me: matching dresses and coats with fake-fur trim, and smocked girly dresses with puffy sashes, and holiday sweaters with fluffy snow-men knitted right into them.

I nod my head.

"So this other little girl and I were supposed to model swimwear together," Mom says. "In other words, bathing suits. And as I said, I wanted to make Mama proud, and I wanted to do a better job than the other little girl who was modeling. You know the type, a little show-offy and stuck-up."

Cynthia, I think, hiding a smile. And probably Lettice Wallingford, too.

"I mean, I *really* wanted to do better," my mom

is saying. "Because when we were introduced, this other little girl looked me up and down like she couldn't believe I was in the same fashion show that she was! Nancy Something, her name was."

I grind my teeth together, wishing that I could bop that nasty little Nancy Something on her stuck-up nose to avenge my tomboy mom.

Sometimes I get tangled up in time.

"And I probably would have done okay," Mom continues, "only the bathing suit Grandmama chose for me had a special long lacy cover-up that went with it. The kind of thing nobody actually wears in real life, especially not a kid."

"Uh-oh," I say, picturing the outfit. Grandmama probably loved it.

"So Nancy and I were weaving down the runway in the glittery flip-flops we had to wear," Mom says, "and when we got to the end of the runway, I was supposed to take off my cover-up, and we were going to twirl around the way models do. And of course I decided to do a *wa-a-ay* better twirl than Miss Nancy. That's all I could think about."

I nod my head, thinking that a better twirl was exactly what *I* would have done.

"But when I was whisking off my cover-up," Mom says, starting to giggle, "some of the lace got snagged on one of the jewels on my flip-flops. And down I went, taking snooty Miss Nancy with me."

"Oh, no," I say.

"Oh, yes! But that's not all, because Nancy was so angry that she shouted out a bad word!"

"Which one?" I ask, and Mom leans over and whispers it in my ear.

"You're kidding," I say in a hushed voice. "Nancy said that word in front of Grandmama? The same Grandmama who scolded you when you were twelve because you kept saying 'yeah'? Not to mention the time she washed your mouth

out with soap because you said 'butt' instead of 'bottom'?"

"Nancy said *her* bad word in front of Grand-mama—and about two hundred other ladies, who were all dressed up," Mom says, still laughing. "So even though the whole fiasco was my fault, and even though Nancy was a whole lot prettier than

I was, I was the one who ended up looking better that day."

"Yes-s-s! You won," I say, pumping my fist in victory the best I can while still lying down. "And no one could be prettier than you," I add loyally.

"Thanks, Emma," Mom says, making a move to get up from the sofa—because by now, it's way past my bedtime.

"No, wait," I say, pressing my head down harder on the flowered pillow to keep her there. "Let's stay here a little bit longer, okay Mom? And listen to the rain? We don't have to talk or anything."

"Okay," Mom says. "We'll think slow for a little while."

"Think slow," I agree. *And dream about tomorrow*, I add silently, crossing my fingers.

9

a Big, Dead Bug

The little kids in kindergarten, first, and second grades were busy with their games day all morning, because our school only has one playground. Our games day, the *real* one, starts right after lunch, which we are just finishing, or trying to finish, because a few of us—me, anyway—are too nervous to eat. I feel as if I have a small flock of cabbage white butterflies in my stomach.

I could barely finish my peanut-butter-and-lettuce-on-a-bagel sandwich.

We will share the still-damp playground with fourth- and fifth-grade kids. Each class will compete on its own, thank goodness, because a lot of those fifth-graders are huge! You could fit two of me inside some of those gigantic boys and still have enough room left for a couple of baby Murphys. Or Murphies, whatever the plural of him is.

But Ms. Sanchez told us that the jumping contest will be fair, because the judges will compare how short you are with how far you can jump.

It's hard to explain, but maybe you get the idea. I sure don't.

"This is gonna be *awful*," Fiona moans as she drops her almost-full lunch sack into the trash. "People shouldn't make other people do dangerous sports when those people have weak ankles."

I sneak a peek at Fiona's ankles. They still look like pink pipe cleaners to me. I sincerely hope Fiona doesn't end up looking like a kindergarten crafts project gone wrong by the end of the afternoon, with her feet pointing every which way. I mean, we aren't best friends or anything, but I don't want her to get *hurt*.

"You'll do okay, Fiona," Annie Pat says, patting her shoulder sympathetically.

Kry Rodgriguez has started doing some stretches and lunges that are making me nervous, because she looks like she's been practicing in secret, too, like Annie Pat and me. So I touch my toes a few times to look like I am also warming up.

"*Psst*," I say to Annie Pat, and she does some stretches, too. But she's acting like she'd rather be someplace else, doing *anything* else.

83

"How do I look?" Heather asks Cynthia, who of course is dressed in a brand-new outfit bought especially for Winter Games Day—even though Ms. Sanchez told us to wear old play clothes and comfortable sneakers.

"You look adorable. But you have some lettuce stuck on your front tooth," Cynthia says, not giving Heather and her purple track suit *or* her tooth a glance. She just *knows* these things, I guess. And Cynthia doesn't bother to ask Heather how *she* looks, because Cynthia knows that her outfit—the matching velvety sweatpants and sweatshirt with big glittery flowers on them—looks cute.

I am wearing red, white, and blue, like I am in the Olympics. I figured it couldn't hurt, and it might help! Jared saluted me this morning, but I just ignored him.

Annie Pat is wearing green pants and a green top. I think she is hoping she will blend in with the grass, and no one will notice her.

I have tried to improve her attitude, but there is only so much a person can do.

Around us, the boys in our class are shoving each other and shouting, which I guess is *their* way of warming up. None of them looks nervous, and no boy is asking any other boy how he looks.

Typical boy behavior. If I had my nature notebook with me, I'd write it down.

Twe-e-e-et! The sound of Ms. Sanchez's whistle pierces through our excited chatter at exactly twelve thirty. "Gather on the playground, third-graders," she calls out, a big smile on her face.

When we get to the playground, which is half grass and half cement or something, lots of parents are waiting, including my mom. I give her a secret wave.

"It's time for Oak Glen School's First Annual Winter Games Day," Ms. Sanchez tells everyone, "and we only have about two hours to finish our three events *and* have the awards ceremony and celebration afterwards, and still get out of school on time. And knowing these boys and girls, *we'll* need every second," she adds, smiling at us kids. "But first, Fiona's father has something special to pass out to all you participating athletes. Mr. Mc-Nulty?"

A big man I have never seen before steps out from behind a bunch of people. He is carrying two boxes, on on top of the other. "Hey, kids," he says, greeting us.

Fiona shrinks back behind Kry, trying to be invisible. She's shy. Even about her own dad, I guess.

"Hey," a few of us reply cautiously.

"I am happy to honor you all today by giving you either a cap or a kerchief to wear and keep, courtesy of McNulty Extermination, located right here in beautiful Oak Glen since 1995 to take care of all your extermination needs," he tells us.

I don't think I have any extermination needs. I'm not sure, actually.

Fiona's dad turns to the grown-ups in the waiting crowd. There are a lot of them standing on the playground, including EllRay's mom with a cute little girl; Mrs. Masterson, holding drooly baby Murphy, of course; my mom; and Mr. Timberlake, the handsome man our beautiful teacher is going to marry someday. We hardly ever get to see him in person.

Mr. McNulty opens the brown cardboard boxes to show us all what is inside.

There is what is supposed to be a big dead bug on each cap and kerchief, but Mr. McNulty's so-called insect only has four legs, not six, so he got it all wrong.

Annie Pat and I know better, so we look at each other and bite back our smiles.

"Cool," a couple of boys murmur, impressed by the dead bug.

"Do we have to pay for them?" Jared asks suspiciously.

"No, son, they're absolutely free," Mr. McNulty says. "Now, who wants what? There's plenty to go around."

"Quickly, children," Ms. Sanchez calls out. "Tick-tock!"

And so we dive on the boxes and start grabbing. Most of the boys want caps, and most of the girls want kerchiefs, but not always. Kry chooses a cap, for instance, and puts it on backwards, making her look even cuter and cooler than before. And Stanley rolls up a kerchief and ties it around his forehead so that he looks like a Native American warrior, which is also cool.

And finally, finally, it is time to begin! I get ready to prove to everyone—especially to my far-away dad—that I am excellent.

This is big. For me, anyway, because there is so much at stake.

I really need to win.

10

the Jumping Contest

The first contest—distance jumping—will be done four kids at a time, Ms. Sanchez tells us, with an adult volunteer measuring each kid's jump. A math wizard will then somehow compare each kid's jump to how tall the kid is, and then they will announce the first- and second-place winners for the boys and for the girls.

"Okay, *jump*!" Ms. Sanchez shouts to the first batch of kids.

Jared tumbles forward on purpose after he leaps, and he scoots his foot a few inches forward when he falls. "That's cheating," EllRay cries, because he was the next kid over, and he had a really good view of the whole thing.

Most of us saw it, in fact, but Jared is not tossed out of Winter Games Day—which is what I would do if I were in charge of things.

Grown-ups are never as strict as kids would be if they had that kind of power, that's what I think.

Instead, Jared's measurer just marks the correct spot. But Jared accidentally-on-purpose shoves EllRay when they are trotting back to join the rest of the class at the edge of the big lawn, and EllRay's dead bug cap falls off.

In the second batch of kids, Fiona springs forward like a little cricket—and then crumples immediately to the grass, clutching at her ankle. But she lifts up her head to peek around and see whether or

The warmer the temperature, the faster crickets chirp.

not everyone has noticed, so I know she's faking.

"Ow–w–w," she moans loudly.

"Oh, Fiona," her mom cries out, streaking so fast across the lawn—like a gazelle!—that I'm glad *she's* not in any of the contests. "Are you okay, my brave little sweetie-pie?"

"I will be tomorrow, probably," Fiona says, sounding courageous and wounded at the same time. "But, oh no!" she exclaims, like the thought just occurred to her. "This means I can't do any more events." And her mom and the volunteer measurer help Fiona limp back to the edge of the lawn, where Heather and Cynthia take over soothing her and staring at her ankle, waiting for it to swell.

Don't hold your breath, that's all I'm saying.

Kevin and Kry and Corey are in the next batch of kids in the jumping contest, and to our combined amazement, Kevin McKinley stuns us all by jumping really, really far. Corey and Kry jump far, too, but that isn't such a surprise, because they're both very good athletes. Nobody gets mad at them for doing well, of course, but for some reason, Jared is furious with Kevin. "What are you tryin' to do, make me look bad?" he asks, sneaking a peek at the parents clustered on the sidelines.

"I'm sorry," a surprised Kevin says. "I don't know what happened."

But he looks just a little bit proud.

I am in the next batch of kids, along with Annie Pat, Cynthia, and Heather. "Good luck," Annie Pat whispers to me.

"Same to you," I say back at her, rocking back and forth in place to get ready.

And then it's my turn, and—*I jump!*

I slice through the cool December air, and when my feet finally hit the earth again, I try to dig in so I won't fall forward like Jared, or collapse in

a little heap like Fiona. And when I look around, I see that I have jumped farther than Annie Pat, Cynthia, *or* Heather.

And I'm the shortest one of them all!

"*Yes-s-s,*" I whisper to myself as the volunteer measures how far I jumped.

Take that, Lettice Wallingford! You don't need to be "just like a daughter" to my dad, because he already *has* a daughter.

My batch of kids trudges back to the rest of the class. "Show-off," Cynthia mutters to me. "You cheated. You practiced, and you—you *tried.*"

"Yeah," Heather says, exchanging outraged glances with Cynthia. "No fair *trying.* Tomboy."

I wait for Annie Pat to come to my defense, but she doesn't say anything. She just looks sad, as if she can see her jumping prize flying away on little white wings—straight out of the awards corner in her room.

I feel bad for her and everything, but I don't

say a word. I'm too busy worrying about my own problems—because of course I don't really know if I've won an actual prize yet. Like I said, they're going to announce the winners as soon as they get it all figured out.

So here is the only score I know so far: Annie Pat is miserable, Fiona is "injured," Jared cheated and is mad at Kevin for doing well, and EllRay and Cynthia are also furious with someone.

Way to go, PTA. We were perfectly happy, until *you* came along.

"Attention, everyone," Ms. Sanchez calls out, waving a clipboard in the air. "I have the winners here!" We all gather around.

"For the boys," she announces, "it's Kevin McKinley in first place, and EllRay Jakes in second place."

"Yay!" almost everyone shouts, especially Kevin and EllRay.

My heart starts to pound.

"And for the girls," Ms. Sanchez calls out, "it's Emma McGraw in first place, and Kry Rodriguez in second place!" People seem to be cheering, but I can barely hear a thing, I am so excited.

I actually won a prize.

χ 11 χ

RUNNING

Next comes running. "There won't be any special calculations for this event," Ms. Sanchez
says. "So you boys and girls will race together—but in two batches. The grown-up volun-
teers will be at the finish line to pick the fastest
two kids in each race," she tells us. "Then there
will be a run-off between the final four kids.
And prizes will go to the two fastest kids, boy
or girl."

"Good luck," I whisper to Annie Pat, who is in
the first batch of kids—but she comes in sixth.

Uh-oh, I think, because I told her she was
going to win for sure.

Kry Rodriguez comes in first in that race, naturally, and Heather—*Heather Patton*, who is so nervous about doing everything perfectly that she can barely even move!—comes in second.

It would have been Corey who came in first or second, considering his champion swimming muscles, but the boys in the first batch of kids were trying so hard to win that they kept tripping each other up and grabbing each other's dead bug caps and Native American warrior kerchiefs and crashing into each other during the race.

There's a lesson there, but I'm not sure what it is.

So now, Corey is mad at Jared and EllRay, and Jared is mad at—well, just about everyone, I guess.

I am in the second batch of kids, and I am hoping there will be another kid-tangle in the middle of the race, because that's my only hope of winning. And that's exactly what happens! Cynthia trips—on a blade of grass, I guess, or on one of her pure white shoelaces—and stumbles into Stanley Washington, who goes down like a giant tree that has just been hit by a bolt of glittery pink-and-lavender lightning. And three other runners pile into them, so there's a mountain of kids yelling and arguing on the lawn as Kevin and I cross the finish line.

Kevin again. But at least I came in second. I get to race in the run-off!

I wish my dad was here to see this.

So now, it's just Kry, Heather, Kevin, and me. The parents—including my mom, who bought a disposable camera at the supermarket just for Winter Games Day—move in close to take a few pictures of this historic event.

I can tell that Annie Pat is totally in shock that she hasn't won any prizes yet, after I got her hopes up and everything. She doesn't even look at me, much less wish me good luck, and that hurts.

Annie Pat is not being a very good sport. I guess it's easier to be a good sport when you're winning than when you're losing, but *still*.

"You better not win," I hear Cynthia whisper to Heather. *"Loser."*

"You better not win, either," Jared tells Kevin. *"Loser."*

That's just not right. Also, it doesn't make any sense, because Heather and Kevin are both doing *great* today—much better than Cynthia and Jared, that's for sure—so how can they be the losers?

But I can't figure that out right now, because it's time to race.

"On your marks, get set, *go*!" Ms. Sanchez shouts in her ladylike way.

And I run—like a deer! Like the wind! Like I am in a swamp, and there is an alligator scrambling after me, its mouth gaping wide!

Kry runs faster, of course, but who cares? I come in second!

"Congratulations," Kry says, and she shakes my sweaty hand.

"Thanks," I manage to say. "Same here." And I am still busy catching my breath as I wonder how I can make things right again with my sad best friend Annie Pat, who is usually the most cheerful person I know.

Or she was until that baby came along.

I feel some of my triumph trickle away, but just a little, because—*I'm actually going to get another prize.* And I can tell my dad all about it next time we e-mail each other.

I don't have to reveal every little detail.

"Congratulations, Kry and Emma," Ms. Sanchez says, beaming a smile our way. My ears are buzzing as I step forward so my mom can take my picture.

I won two prizes, even though one was for coming in second. I cannot believe it. I have officially doubled the number of prizes in my room!

"Now, gather 'round, children," Ms. Sanchez is

saying. "Because it's time for our final fun event, and then we'll all enjoy the lovely refreshments your parents have been kind enough to bring. Nice healthy carrot sticks, and cherry tomatoes, and apple slices, and string cheese, for those of you who are not lactose-intolerant, and a pitcher of nice cold water. But first, I need you to pay attention, because this might seem a little complicated."

✕ 12 ✕
the Good Old-fashioned three-Legged Race

"Listen carefully, girls and boys," Ms. Sanchez calls out as we are herded into a group by Mr. Timberlake and a couple of the parents. "This last event is the good old-fashioned three-legged race," she says, clasping her hands together. Her engagement ring flashes in the afternoon sunlight. "That means two kids run together as partners," she explains, "and each kid has one leg tied to his or her partner's leg. So each set of partners ends up running with three legs. Get it? And it's not as easy as it sounds. You're going to have to cooperate with each other."

Uh, wrong kids, wrong day, Ms. Sanchez. Most of us can't even stand to look at each other by now. Take me and Annie Pat, for instance.

And—a *little* complicated? Try a lot complicated!

"This sounds dangerous," Fiona says. But handsome Mr. Timberlake talked to her in private, and he tied a dead bug kerchief around her still-skinny ankle, and she was so thrilled she agreed to participate in this last event.

"Now, you'll all run at once," Ms. Sanchez tells us. "And I'll assign the partners, to save time. Ell-Ray, you run with Fiona. Heather, you'll run with Cynthia. Jared, I want you to run with Stanley. And Kry, you run with Kevin."

Uh-oh. She's pairing up kids totally at random.

"And Emma," Ms. Sanchez says, "you and Annie Pat will run together."

Oh, no. Annie Pat? Who didn't even wish me

luck? Annie Pat, who is acting like she's sorry I am winning even though she knows why I need to?

Annie Pat raises her hand. "Ms. Sanchez? Ms. Sanchez?" she says, pleading.

She is going to beg to be assigned to someone else.

I could never forgive her for this, so I will beg *first*. "Ms. Sanchez?" I call out, waving my arm wildly in the air.

"No time to chat, ladies," Ms. Sanchez says, shooting us a simmer-down look. "In fact," she adds, "I'd like you to give us all a quick demonstration of how to run this race, after one of the parents— Mrs. Jakes?—ties your inside legs together."

This doesn't take as long as I wish it would.

Annie Pat and I refuse to look at each other.

"Go!" Ms. Sanchez shouts.

And I start running, but Annie Pat is still adjusting her green shirt. "Ow!" we both yell, falling onto the grass in a big wad of tangled brown hair, two red pigtails, three legs, and four arms.

Then we try to stand up, which is even worse, and nearly everyone on the sidelines is laughing at us. Even baby Murphy! My mom tries to hide her giggles and look encouraging. She gives me a thumbs-up.

"Listen," I mutter to Annie Pat. "Just go when I say go."

"No," Annie Pat says, stomping her outside foot. "You go when *I* say go, for a change."

Did I mention before that Annie Pat can be stubborn? Or even *impossible?*

Well, I didn't know until three minutes ago!

And I start to run, dragging Annie Pat behind me—but I'm not getting very far.

"Wait, wait, wait," Annie Pat yells from down on the grass, reaching up to grab hold of my patriotic shirt. "We've gotta plan what we're doing." She struggles to her feet.

Lots of people on the sidelines are shouting out suggestions, but we don't listen to them, because I guess this has to be between Annie Pat and me.

"Plan it like how?" I ask.

"Like outside legs, inside legs," Annie Pat says. "Outside, inside."

"Okay," I tell her. "I get to choose how we start, though. *Outside!*" I cry out, and take a giant leap forward with my outside leg.

But Annie Pat just stands there. No matter how

many people shout at us, including Ms. Sanchez, Annie Pat will not be hurried. "All those in favor of starting with your outside leg, say 'aye,'" she says to the air around me.

I wait for her to vote, so I can vote the same way. Because otherwise, we may as well just *move* here! There is no bossing Annie Pat Masterson around. I have now learned this the hard way.

And slowly, slowly, Annie Pat raises her hand.

So I raise my hand, too.

"Those opposed?" Annie Pat asks, looking around—which makes me want to shake her until her teeth rattle, because *who else is there?*

But I don't shake her, and no one is opposed, so Annie Pat's motion passes.

"Well, maybe we'd better get going," I tell Annie Pat casually, as if a bazillion eyes aren't watching our every move. "You say when."

"Okay. Hook your arm over my shoulder," Annie Pat says. "*When!*" she cries. "Outside leg, inside legs. Outside, inside!" And once we get the rhythm right, we start flying, and laughing, and we're as good as gold.

And that's better than a silver cup any day of the week!

X X X

It is time for the *real* three-legged race, and all the kids in my class are lined up at the starting line, including Heather and Cynthia, Kry and Kevin, Jared and Stanley, EllRay and Fiona, and Annie Pat and me.

Tied-up, is more like it!

"I hope I don't make you lose, Emma," Annie Pat whispers just before Ms. Sanchez blows her whistle. "I wish you could do this without me. I know you really need to win, because of your dad and everything."

"Don't worry about it," I say. "I wouldn't want to do it without you even if I could."

I wish I could tell her that I think we already won, but I can't exactly figure out how to explain it.

Twe-e-e-et!

"Go," Annie Pat and I say together, and off we lurch, *swing-bump, swing-bump, swing-bump,* across the lawn, laughing so hard we can barely run.

Kry and Kevin take the lead early, and they look like they're going to keep it, streaking across the grass like the fastest three-legged animal in the world.

But then EllRay and the miraculously cured Fiona whiz by Annie Pat and me like a three-legged cheetah, and I wonder if *they'll* be the winners.

Whatever happened to Fiona's weak ankles? What a faker!

Jared and Stanley struggle to catch up with EllRay and Fiona. They thump across the lawn like

A hippo can run faster than a man.

a wounded—but cooperative—hippopotamus.

And somewhere behind us, I can hear Cynthia shouting at poor Heather, whose only goal in life so far has been to make Cynthia Harbison happy.

Good luck with that, as Cynthia herself would say.

In my opinion, Cynthia's jealous that Heather has already won a prize, and she, Cynthia, has not. Cynthia doesn't know a good friend when she has one!

But maybe Cynthia's just shouting because she has never cooperated with anyone a day in her life.

Either way, they're both doomed.

Sooner or later, we all cross the finish line.

"And it's a two-way tie," Ms. Sanchez shouts above all the cheering. "Kevin McKinley and Kry Rodriguez, and Fiona McNulty and EllRay Jakes!"

❧ 13 ❧

awards

"Over here, everyone," Ms. Sanchez calls out over by the picnic table that has been set up on the playground, and Mr. Timberlake helps round us up from wherever it is we are being photographed and congratulated—even the kids like Jared, Stanley, Cynthia, and Heather, who didn't win anything but who are still grinning and posing like crazy.

EllRay's mom has been photographing him again and again, and his cute little sister is almost glued to his side, she is so proud and happy. My mom takes a few pictures of me, then Mrs. Masterson takes Annie Pat's picture while my mom holds a drooling Murphy Masterson to her chest.

Seeing my mom do this makes me feel a little funny, but it also makes me daydream again about what it would be like to have a baby brother or sister. If that ever happens, I just hope it's Mom who has the baby, and not my dad and Annabelle!

I don't know why, but that's the way I feel about it.

"Gather around," Ms. Sanchez says again, and she blows her whistle to get our attention. "There are snacks waiting, and it's time to hand out the awards."

That gets our attention.

"As you remember," Ms. Sanchez says, glancing down at her clipboard, "the winners of our jumping event were Kevin and EllRay in first and second places for the boys, and Emma and Kry in first and second places for the girls."

There is clapping and cheering as she hands out gold stars with blue ribbons hanging from them for first place, and silver stars with red ribbons hanging from them for second place.

I try to look modest as I clutch my gold star, but it's hard.

"And for event number two, running, we have Kry winning first place," Ms. Sanchez says, "and Emma winning second place."

There is more applause, and now I have a gold star *and* a silver star.

Yahoo!

"And finally, as you recall," Ms. Sanchez says, "for our three-legged race, we have a two-way tie for first place. Kry, Kevin, EllRay, and Fiona, please step forward to receive your awards."

And we all clap like crazy as she hands out four more gold stars.

"So that means," Ms. Sanchez calls out over the uproar, "that EllRay, Kevin, and Kry have each won two first-place awards this afternoon. And Fiona and Emma have each won one first-place award. And special recognition must also go to Kry Rodriguez, both for her total of three—*three!*—awards and for her overall good sportsmanship today, and during the week leading up to this event. Kry, will you please step forward so we can all thank you?"

"I would have been nice, too, if I knew it was gonna *count*," Annie Pat and I hear Cynthia tell Heather as Kry receives an extra-fancy gold-and-silver star from Ms. Sanchez and everyone takes her picture.

"Me, too," Heather says. "Like that's so *fair*."

"But I guess I wasn't a very good sport, either," Annie Pat admits to me as we scoop up dip with our carrot sticks during the celebration following Winter Games Day.

"You were okay," I say.

This is what's known as "a little white lie," but sometimes, that's the way to go.

Also, I know that *I* was probably only a good sport because I was winning.

"No, it's not okay," Annie Pat says, grabbing

some string cheese for the two of us before the boys hog it all. "I didn't stick up for you when Cynthia and Heather called you a show-off and a tomboy, and I didn't say 'good luck' before you ran, even after you said it to me. And by the time we got to the three-legged race demonstration, I actually wanted you to lose. So there! That's how bad a sport I was."

"You were probably just tired," I say, trying to give her a good excuse. "I think Murphy is kind of messing you up lately, crying all night and everything."

"It's not his fault he yells so much and is using up my mom," Annie Pat says with a sigh, peeling off a thready strip of cheese. "Teeth pop into a baby's mouth whether he wants them to or not, and when that happens, he's just gotta cry—even if his sister has a big race the next day. It's just nature."

"I guess," I say, thinking about everything that happened this afternoon. "Do you really think I'm bossy?" I ask Annie Pat shyly. "Like, telling you what to do and when to do it all the time, like you said when we were demonstrating that race?"

Annie Pat laughs, sounding embarrassed. "You're not as bad as Cynthia, that's for sure," she assures me, pointing toward the snack table.

Cynthia is over by the bowl of dip as we speak, guarding it against double-dippers. "That's just *disgusting*!" Cynthia shouts at Jared, who has just scooped his actual fingers through the bowl—and licked them.

"Yeah! *Yuck*," Heather yells, backing Cynthia up.

Heather has a very full reservoir of forgiveness, when it comes to Cynthia.

"Well, that's something, I guess, to be not as bad as Cynthia," I say to Annie Pat. "Look," I add, feeling sort of awkward, "I want to talk to you."

"Okay," Annie Pat says, listening.

"I want to say that I think being a good friend is just as important as winning an award for jumping or running," I tell her shyly. "Maybe it's *more* important. And you're my really good friend, Annie Pat."

"Even though I wanted you to lose the three-legged race?" she asks.

"That was only for a second," I remind her. "I never said you were *perfect*."

Annie Pat giggles.

I take a deep breath. "So anyway," I continue, "I want this gold star to be yours, in honor of us being such excellent friends." And I give her one of my stars—a little slowly, but I do it.

And it's my best star, too.

Annie Pat stares hard at the gold star that is now resting in my hand, as if picturing it practically glowing in her awards corner. "No-o-o," she says slowly. "It's got your name on it, see? *'Emma McGraw, First Place, Jumping.'* And what about your dad?"

"Number one, I can change what's on the award," I assure her. "I have construction paper and a glue stick and glitter markers at home, don't

I? And number two, my dad's not even here to see the award, so what difference does it make if I actually have it up on my wall or not?"

"Yeah. You still won," Annie Pat says, thinking it over. "And you can still tell him about it when you guys e-mail each other," she adds. "But—what about your mom? Won't she be mad if you give away your best award?"

I look over at my mom. She still has baby Murphy in her arms, but he has fallen fast asleep on her shoulder. It looks like she's holding a little sack of potatoes with red hair on top. Mom is laughing quietly, and talking to a bunch of the other moms, but then she glances over at me and waves. *"I love you,"* she tells me, silently mouthing the words.

I smile at her and wave back. "My mother won't care," I tell Annie Pat. "In fact, she'll probably say it was the exact right thing to do."

14

aLmost Like a ɒauɢнteʀ

"Why did you want to win so badly yesterday, sweetie?" Mom asks me the next night, Saturday, when she is tucking me in. It is raining again, but I feel nice and cozy.

"Because I couldn't afford to lose," I confess. "No one could. Not with all the parents there."

"*What?*" my mom asks, obviously trying to get it.

"It's true," I tell her. "Annie Pat *always* wins something, no matter what she does, so how could she start losing all of a sudden? You should see all her prizes, Mom! And Cynthia Harbison couldn't risk losing a contest in front of her mom, because her mom is always saying how perfect she is. And I don't know why," I add, "but Heather can't stand to see Cynthia lose *anything*. And I think Fiona was so freaked out about the *idea* of not winning that she didn't even want to try."

"Hmm," Mom says, frowning.

"And the boys were even more worried than the girls were about losing," I continue eagerly, wanting her to understand. "I mean, it's not right that Stanley has to be embarrassed in public, just because he's too chunky to win a race. His parents think he's good at everything! How much pressure is *that*? And Jared needs *us* to think he's so great, for some reason, but only Kevin really thinks Jared is. *So great*, I mean. And you can tell that EllRay hates being short. He shouldn't have to be a loser, too, on top of that."

"But EllRay wasn't a loser," Mom reminds me. "And you can lose a contest without being a *loser*," she adds. "In fact, you can even end up a winner."

"How?" I ask drowsily, even though Annie Pat and I already know.

"Well, by trying your best, for one thing," my mom tells me. "And by being a good sport—like Kry Rodriguez was—whether you win *or* lose. But why was winning so important to *you*?"

"Because of Daddy," I say instantly, shutting

my eyes. "I wanted to have something really good to tell him when I e-mail him tomorrow. You know, so he remembers how much he loves me."

"He doesn't need to be reminded of that, Emma," Mom tells me in her softest voice.

"I know, I know," I say. "But I'm here, and he's there, Mom, in London, England. With *Annabelle*. And with Lettice Wallingford coming over all the time, eating cupcakes with him," I add, my voice a mumble.

"Who in the world is Lettice Wallingford?" my mom asks.

"She's this perfect girl who is almost like a daughter to Annabelle," I say, not wanting to meet Mom's confused gaze. "She's her niece or something. Lettice just won a silver cup for horseback riding."

"A silver cup. Goodness," Mom echoes, her eyes wide. I guess she's impressed, too.

"But I won *two* prizes, didn't I?" I remind her—

and myself. "And maybe I would have won three, if everything had gone the way I wanted it to. Can I tell my dad about the prizes I *might* have won?"

"I think you should tell him the whole story," my mom says quietly. "Starting with your feelings about Lettice Wallingford, and going on from there—to Winter Games Day, and the three events, and you giving your gold star away to Annie Pat, which I think was the most important event of the entire afternoon. He'll want to know everything, sweetie."

"But that would take forever to write," I point out, trying to sound reasonable. "Do you know how long that e-mail would be? I'd have to start writing it *yesterday*!"

Also, I admit to myself, I don't want to write too much and accidentally tell my dad any bad stuff about me—like how I was kind of glad that Jared tripped up Corey during the running event, and that Cynthia crashed into Stanley and they both fell down. I can't take that chance, not with him being so far away from me—and so close to Lettice Wallingford.

"He'll think I'm a loser," I whisper, thinking of fabulous Lettice and her silver cup. She probably carries it with her everywhere she goes.

"Never," Mom tells me. "He's your father, Emma. And even though he's far away, he wants to know the truth about everything that's going on in your life, both the good things and the bad. Nothing is ever going to change the way he feels about you, darling. He'll know you're still his wonderful girl who wins sometimes and loses sometimes. You still love *him*, don't you? Even though he's not around?"

"More than ever," I say.

"Well, he feels the same way about you," Mom tells me. "Your father doesn't expect you to be perfect, Emma. But, like me, he always wants you to try your best, and to be kind. That's why I'm so proud of you, and that's why he will be, too."

"I'm almost like a daughter to him," I say shyly.

"Oh, Emma!" Mom says, laughing, and she reels me in for a great big hug.

Excellent.